Storm Treasure

A story in a
familiar setting

First published in 2005 by
Franklin Watts
96 Leonard Street
London
EC2A 4XD

Franklin Watts Australia
Level 17/207 Kent Street
Sydney
NSW 2000

A CIP catalogue record for this book is available
from the British Library.

ISBN 0 7496 6136 4 (hbk)
ISBN 0 7496 6142 9 (pbk)

Series Editor: Jackie Hamley
Series Advisors: Dr Barrie Wade, Dr Hilary Minns
Design: Peter Scoulding

Printed in China

The publishers would like to thank Douglas Herdson
at the National Marine Aquarium, Plymouth, UK.

For Greta, with love – N.U.

Storm Treasure

Written by
Anne Adeney

Illustrated by
Natascia Ugliano

W
FRANKLIN WATTS
LONDON•SYDNEY

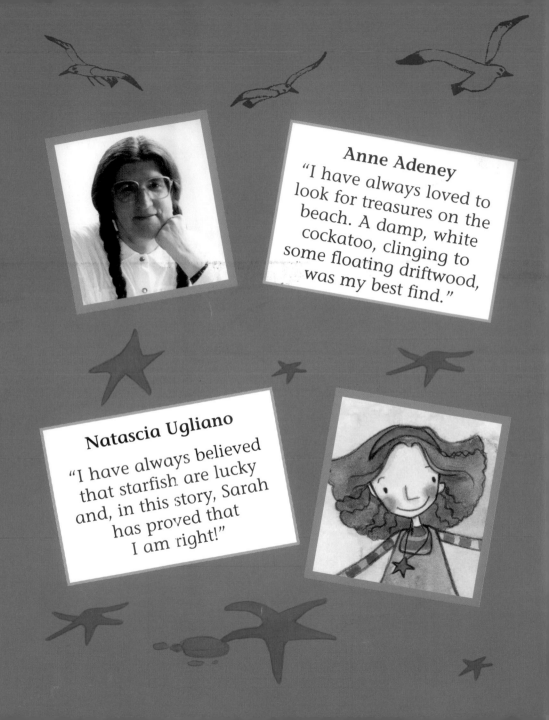

Anne Adeney
"I have always loved to look for treasures on the beach. A damp, white cockatoo, clinging to some floating driftwood, was my best find."

Natascia Ugliano
"I have always believed that starfish are lucky and, in this story, Sarah has proved that I am right!"

Sarah lived by the beach with

Mum and Grandad.

In summer, it was a very busy place.

In winter, Sarah and Grandad
loved the empty beach.

They often saw starfish in the rock
pools. Sarah loved to see their
orange bodies and five strong arms.

"Starfish eat mussels and barnacles that grow on the rocks," said Grandad. "They need to stay in the water to find food."

11

Grandad was good at skimming
flat stones across the sea.

His stones bounced six or seven
times before they sank.

Sarah and Grandad walked
for hours along the beach.

They always found things
that the sea had washed up.

Grandad called them flotsam and jetsam. Sarah called them storm treasure. She liked to take them home in her wheelbarrow.

17

One winter night, there was a big storm.

Next day, Grandad and Mum
had lots of things to mend.

Later, Sarah went to look for storm treasure on the beach. She was surprised to see what treasure the storm had left!

There were lots of starfish, right
at the top of the beach.

Sarah remembered that starfish
need to be in the water to find food.

She knew they would die
at the top of the beach.

Sarah had never picked up a starfish before, but she didn't want them to die.

Sarah picked up all the starfish
she could see.

She wheeled them down
to the water.

Then she carefully put a starfish
into each rock pool.

Sarah smiled as she saw
them sink one by one into
the water.

Today's storm treasures were
safe in their homes again.

Notes for parents and teachers

READING CORNER has been structured to provide maximum support for new readers. The stories may be used by adults for sharing with young children. Primarily, however, the stories are designed for newly independent readers, whether they are reading these books in bed at night, or in the reading corner at school or in the library.

Starting to read alone can be a daunting prospect. READING CORNER helps by providing visual support and repeating words and phrases, while making reading enjoyable. These books will develop confidence in the new reader, and encourage a love of reading that will last a lifetime!

If you are reading this book with a child, here are a few tips:

1. Make reading fun! Choose a time to read when you and the child are relaxed and have time to share the story.

2. Encourage children to reread the story, and to retell the story in their own words, using the illustrations to remind them what has happened.

3. Give praise! Remember that small mistakes need not always be corrected.

READING CORNER covers three grades of early reading ability, with three levels at each grade. Each level has a certain number of words per story, indicated by the number of bars on the spine of the book, to allow you to choose the right book for a young reader:

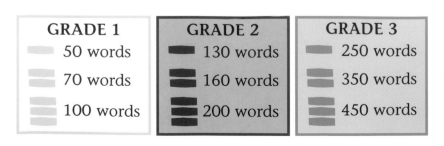

GRADE 1	GRADE 2	GRADE 3
50 words	130 words	250 words
70 words	160 words	350 words
100 words	200 words	450 words